Vampire School

Casketball

Capers

Northumberland County Council	
3 0132 02101696 4	
Askews & Holts	Feb-2012
JF	£4.99

For Theo and Tara
P.B.
For my family
C.H.

First published in Great Britain in 2010
by Boxer Books Limited.

www.boxerbooks.com

Based on an original idea by Chris Harrison
Text copyright © 2010 Peter Bently
Illustrations copyright © 2010 Chris Harrison

The illustrations were prepared using biro and watercolour paints
The text is set in Blackmoor Plain and Adobe Caslon

ISBN 978-1-907152-20-7

1 3 5 7 9 10 8 6 4 2

Printed in Great Britain

All of our papers are sourced from managed forests and renewable resources.

Vampire School

Casketball Capers

Written by Peter Bently

Illustrated by Chris Harrison

Boxer Books

Contents

Chapter 1
School Time

Lee Price was nine years old. He lived with his mum and dad in an ordinary house in an ordinary street and, like most nine-year-olds, he went to school every day.

Or rather, every night.

Because St. Orlok's Primary School was no ordinary school, and Lee was no ordinary boy.

St. Orlok's was a school for young vampires.

Young vampires like Lee Price.

At St. Orlok's, Lee and his friends learnt to do all the things that vampires do.

Like cloak-swishing...

Scary staring...

Tying a
bow tie...

Losing your reflection...

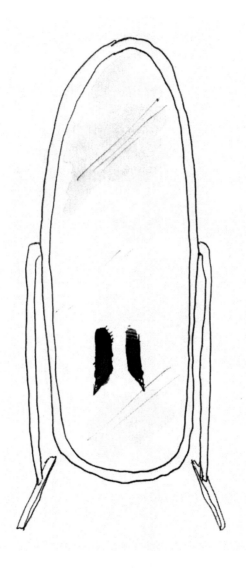

Looking after your teeth...

And cooking without garlic.

Early one night, Lee's mum called up the stairs, just like she did every evening.

"Lee! Time to get up for school!"

Lee blinked sleepily in the bright moonlight.

"Aw," he groaned. "Just five more minutes!"

"No, dear. It's already ten past eight. If you don't get up now you'll be late."

Lee got dressed and went down to the kitchen for breakfast.

Dad was getting ready to go
to work. He patted Lee on the
head.

"Cheerio, Lee," he said.
"Have a good night at school.

And good
luck in
the match.
Don't let
any of those
werewolves
near the
casket!"

"Thanks, Dad, I won't," grinned Lee, gulping down a mouthful of blood orange juice.

Lee was on the St. Orlok's school casketball team. Casketball was the vampire version of basketball. Today they were playing in the Junior Inter-School Series against the werewolves of Chaney Street First School.

With a little *POP!* Dad changed into a bat and fluttered out of the kitchen window.

Then Lee remembered.

"Hey, Mum! We're starting bat lessons today! We're learning how to turn into bats and how to fly. I can't wait!"

"Come on then," said Mum, looking at her watch. "Got your casketball kit? Good. Now put your cloak on and nip upstairs to comb your hair. And don't forget to brush your fangs."

Chapter 2
Bat Lessons

Mum left Lee at the gates of St. Orlok's. She gave him a peck on the cheek, said, "See you at half past three," then with a *POP!* she turned into a bat and flapped back home.

Lee ran to join Bella
Williams and Billy Pratt, his
best friends at school. They
were all in Miss Gargoyle's
class and very excited about
their first bat lesson.

"Being a bat will be great," said Lee. "We'll be able to fly to the tops of trees instead of climbing them."

"No way!" said Billy, who didn't like heights. "The best thing will be flying *really* fast."

"Did you know that there are over a thousand types of bat?" said Bella. "Mum bought me a book about it. I wonder what sort we'll turn into..."

"Don't be daft," said Lee. "*Vampire* bats, of course."

Lee, Billy and Bella reached their classroom just as Miss Gargoyle was about to take the register.

"Settle down now, children," said Miss Gargoyle. "Tonight I will show you one of the most important vampire skills – how to turn into a bat!"

The children all gathered
round.

"First of all, you must really
think hard about being a bat,"
said Miss Gargoyle. She closed
her eyes.

"My arms are not arms but bat wings. My legs are little bat legs. My body is small and furry. My head is a bat's head with big bat ears. Got that?"

"Yes, Miss Gargoyle," chorused the class.

"Next, I say these words to myself –

I'm a bat, a bat is me,
A bat is all I want to be."

With a soft *POP!* Miss Gargoyle changed into a little brown bat flapping in front of the blackboard.

"See?" squeaked Miss Gargoyle. "To change back, just say –

*Pointy fangs
    and swishing cape,
It's time to take on
    vampire shape.*"

With another *POP!* Miss Gargoyle changed back into a vampire.

"Remember, don't *POP!* too loudly or Fangless people might hear," she said. "Right, now you all have a go."

Lee, Bella and Billy soon found that changing into a bat wasn't as easy as it looked.

At first, Lee only
managed to change
his arms...

...and Bella changed
everything except
her head.

Billy changed
himself into a *cat*...

and then a *rat*...

But finally there was a *POP!*
and suddenly Lee was flapping
around the room.

"I did it! I did it!" he
squeaked. "I'm a bat!"

Chapter 3
Boris the Bat

By the time the bell rang for
lunch break, the classroom
was full of little bats, giggling
with glee.

"Well done, class!" said Miss
Gargoyle. "After lunch we'll
have a go at hanging upside
down. There'll be a little time
before the werewolves arrive
for the casketball match."

Lee and his friends gobbled down lunch and ran outside. They couldn't wait to practise turning into bats.

It was a lot trickier without Miss Gargoyle there to help. First of all, Lee's left half became a bat but his right half stayed the same...

Bella turned into a huge ball of bat fur...

And Billy turned into a *bag*.

But at last they managed it. With a *POP! POP! POP!* they were all fluttering around the playground.

"Come on," said Bella. "Let's all play hide and seek! I'll count to twenty." She shut her eyes.

"One, two, three – "

Quick as a flash, Billy darted off out of sight. Lee looked around for a hiding place. On a window ledge? No, Bella would spot him too easily.

"Four, five, six – "

Inside the school bins? Poo!
Too smelly!

"Seven, eight, nine – "

'Aha!' thought Lee. 'Behind
the school gates!'

But Billy was already hiding
there.

"Go away, Lee!" he said.
"You'll give us both away!"

"Ten, eleven, twelve – "

"Yikes!" cried Lee. "This is harder than I thought!"

"Thirteen, fourteen, fifteen – "

DONG! The school clock struck midnight.

'That's it!' Lee thought suddenly. 'The clock tower!

Where better for a bat to hide than in a belfry?'

"Sixteen, seventeen, eighteen –"

Lee made it to the tower just in time. As Bella cried, "Nineteen, twenty. Coming, ready or not!" he darted through a hole in the school clock – and bumped straight into another bat.

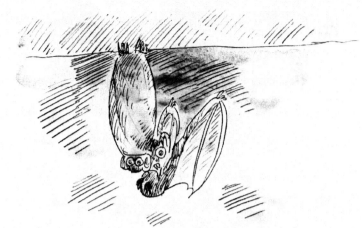

"Hey, watch where you're going!" said the bat.

"Sorry!" said Lee. He didn't recognise the other bat so he said, "My name's Lee. What's yours?"

"Boris," grunted the bat gruffly.

"Hi, Boris," smiled Lee. "I'm in Miss Gargoyle's class. Which class are you in?"

"Class?" snorted Boris. "Oh, I'm not one of you silly vampire kids. I'm a *real* bat."

"A real bat!" gasped Lee. "Wow! Cool!"

"That's right," said Boris. "You vampires think you're so clever, turning into bats and all. But you can't do half the things a *proper* bat can. Like this!"

Boris folded his wings and dropped like a stone all the way down to the bottom of the tower.

"Hey!" yelled Lee in terror. "Watch out!"

Boris was just about to hit
the ground when he opened
his wings and pulled up at
the last moment. He fluttered
back up to Lee.

"See?" said Boris. "Now off you go and play with those vampire friends of yours. Belfries are for *real* bats."

"But I'm supposed to be hiding," said Lee. "Can't I stay for a bit? I'd *love* to learn some real bat tricks. They're so cool!"

Boris shrugged. "All right. Just for a little while though. I don't want any of my mates to think I hang out with *vampires*."

Lee was delighted. With Boris to help, he had a go at divebombing,

looping the loop,

and dodging things with his
eyes shut.

"Not bad," said Boris with a grin. "Not bad at all. For a vampire."

Just then the school clock struck one.

"Yikes!" cried Lee.

"That was loud!" Then he remembered. "One o'clock! I'll be late for class! See you soon, Boris. And thanks for the tricks!"

Chapter 4
Growler the Fouler

Lee zoomed out of the belfry and back to his classroom. The others had already started to practise hanging upside down.

"Come along now, Lee

Price!" said Miss Gargoyle sternly. "You're late. Don't hang about. Or rather *do* hang about. Hurry up and find an empty place."

Billy and Bella had saved Lee a space on the curtains.

"Where were you hiding?" whispered Bella.

"Yeah, we couldn't find you anywhere," said Billy.

"I was in

the clock tower," said Lee. "I met this real bat called Boris. He's dead cool."

He was about to tell them more when they heard a *toot-toot* and saw a bus driving into the school gates.

"Look," said Bella. "The werewolves are here!"

"Aha!" said Miss Gargoyle, fluttering over to the window. "Lee, Billy and Bella, you'd better go and get ready for the match. The rest of us will be along to cheer you on!"

By the time the St. Orlok's
team had got changed, the
Chaney Street werewolves
were already out on the
field warming up under the
floodlights.

Lee jogged over to Ollie
Talbot, his friend on the
werewolf team.

"Hi, Ollie," he said. "Guess
what? We had our first bat
lessons today!"

"Cool!" said Ollie. "So this means you're even battier than usual."

"Ha-ha, very funny," groaned Lee. Ollie was always making terrible jokes.

Just then, a big werewolf pointed at them and sneered.

"Uh-oh, here comes Robbie Growler," sighed Ollie. "Just ignore him."

"What, Growler the Fouler?" said Lee.

"That's him," said Ollie. "The dirtiest player in Chaney Street. He's our new Shooter."

There were two Shooters on each team, and they scored most of the goals. The vampire Shooters were Bella, who was tall for her age, and another girl called Naz Patel in the year above.

As well as the Shooters, there were three Dodgers, whose main job was to keep the ball away from their own casket and pass it, dribble it, roll it or throw it into the hands of the Shooters. Billy, who was small and very fast, was a brilliant Dodger.

The sixth player on each side was the Ghoulkeeper, who defended the casket. That was Lee's job.

"Hey, Ollie," cried Growler. "Why are you talking to that sucker, eh? Geddit? Sucker! Hur-hur-hur!" He loped off up the field, sniggering stupidly.

Lee was furious. He picked up a stick.

"Lee, no!" gasped Ollie.

"He'll make mincemeat out of you!"

Lee grinned.

"Don't worry, I'm not going to hit him. Just watch."

Growler turned around and snarled. Lee whistled as if he was calling a dog, then threw the stick towards him.

"Here boy!" he called. "Good boy! Fetch!"

The vampires all laughed, and so did Ollie and most of the other werewolves – when Growler wasn't looking.

Bella and Billy were in fits. Growler glared at Lee.

"Come here, you little squirt," he rumbled. "I just fancy a snack."

"Now, now!" said Mr Tut, the mummy referee. "There'll be none of that, please! I want a good clean game!"

Chapter 5
Mr Tut in a Tangle

The two casketball teams took up their positions. Mr Tut blew his whistle and the game began.

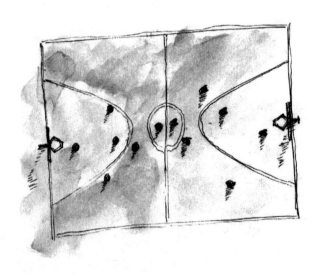

Billy got the ball and nipped past the three werewolf Dodgers before bouncing it to Naz Patel.

The vampires cheered Naz on as she charged towards the Chaney Street casket – with Growler close behind.

"Go on, Naz!" cried Lee.

Then he noticed that Growler kept looking at Mr Tut, who was fiddling with a loose bandage on his head.

'Growler's up to something,' thought Lee.

He was right. Just then, the loose bandage slipped over the referee's eyes and Growler grinned.

"Watch it, Naz!" cried Bella, who was already up by the Chaney Street casket.

It was too late. While Mr Tut was busy with his bandages, Growler grabbed the back of Naz's shirt and punched the ball out of her hand.

"It's a foul, ref!" cried the vampires.

But it was no good. Mr Tut hadn't seen a thing.

"Thanks for the ball, sucker," cackled Growler, as Naz stumbled and fell to the ground. "Hur-hur-hur!"

Growler headed off towards
the vampire casket.

"Stop him, Billy!" cried Lee,
as Growler closed in on the St.
Orlok's Dodgers.

But the huge werewolf snarled
at Billy so fiercely that he leapt
out of his way in terror.

There was nothing now between Growler and the casket except Lee. Growler made a move to the left, and Lee followed him. But then the werewolf quickly swung the other way, pounced high off the ground – and slammed the ball into the casket.

The werewolf supporters all
cried, "Goal!" and bayed and
whooped in delight. Five
points to Chaney Street!

So it went on. Every time
Mr Tut's loose bandage slipped
over his eyes, Growler pushed,
pulled or tripped up one of the
vampire players and kicked or
punched the ball out of their
hands.

By half-time the vampires
still hadn't scored.

"It's no use," moaned Lee
as the teams went off for
the break. "We don't stand a
chance with Growler on their
side."

"I know," agreed Bella. "It's
not fair. He's such a cheat."

"Yeah, and the ref is as blind as a bat," said Billy.

'Blind as a bat,' thought Lee. 'I wonder...'

With a *POP!* Lee suddenly turned into a bat.

"Back in a sec!" he said, and flitted off.

"Hey, where is he going?" said Bella.

"Dunno," said Billy. "Looks like he's heading for the clock tower..."

Chapter 6
Boris to the Rescue

In the second half of the
game, St. Orlok's managed to
stop the werewolves scoring
again, but Growler made sure
that no one got anywhere near
the Chaney Street casket.

Even when he wasn't cheating
he was so big and fierce that
most of the vampires were
terrified of him.

One minute from the end of the match, it looked like the werewolves were going to win – and then Billy got the ball and niftily bounced it to Bella.

"Go on, Bella!" cried Lee,
as Bella zipped past several
werewolves.

"Watch out for Growler!"
yelled Billy.

Sure enough, Mr Tut
was soon fiddling with the
flapping bandages over his
eyes. Growler saw his chance

to cheat and thundered down
the pitch after Bella. But just
as he reached her, a small
black thing dived out of the
sky and grabbed hold of Mr
Tut's loose bandage.

It was Boris the bat!

Boris lifted the bandage just in time for Mr Tut to see Growler giving Bella a great shove. With a SPLAT! she landed on her bottom in a patch of mud.

"Hur-hur-hur!" chuckled Growler, running off with the ball. "So long, sucker – eh? What?"

Mr Tut was blowing his whistle.

"Foul! One penalty point to the vampires and a free throw at the casket!"

"Nice one, Boris!" grinned Lee.

"Don't mention it," said Boris.

Growler pointed angrily at Boris. "Hey, ref!" he cried. "One of them's changed into a bat!"

Turning into a bat was against the rules. Any vampire caught doing it would be sent off at once.

"Nonsense!" said Mr Tut. "Vampire bats have got big fangs. And besides, we'd have heard it go *POP*. This is a *real* bat. And very useful it is too. Play on!"

Suddenly the vampires had
a chance. Growler glared at
Bella as she stepped up for the
free throw. She jogged into
the scoring zone, leapt – and
neatly lobbed the ball into the
Chaney Street casket. Five
more points to the vampires!

Then, amid the cheers of the vampires, Mr Tut blew the final whistle.

The score was St. Orlok's 6, Chaney Street 5. St. Orlok's had won!

POP! POP! POP! POP!

Within seconds, dozens of joyful vampires were turning into bats and flying over the field in glee.

"I'm glad we didn't win," said Ollie Talbot as the two teams left the field. "We didn't deserve to after all of

Growler's cheating."

"Yeah," said Billy. "But where did that bat come from?"

Lee swished open his cape. Inside, hanging upside down, was Boris.

"Meet my new friend, Boris," said Lee.

"Hi, Boris," said Billy.

"Thanks for helping," said Bella.

"Well, I *do* hate cheating,"
said Boris. "That's something
a bat would *never* do."

"*Or* a vampire," said Lee.
"It's just not fair."

Boris grinned. "I suppose
you vampires are all right,
really," he chuckled. "Even if
you aren't *real* bats."

"Not real bats, eh?" laughed Lee. "We'll soon see about that."

Lee gave Billy and Bella a funny look. They nodded. Then, with a *POP! POP! POP!* they all turned into bats.

"Right, Boris," cried Lee. "We'll race you to the clock tower. Last one there's a zombie!"

And the four bats zoomed off, laughing and giggling, high above the roofs of St. Orlok's Primary.

The End

Hungry for more?
Get your teeth into the next Vampire School adventure

Vampire School
Ghoul Trip

Lee, Billy and Bella and the rest of Miss Gargoyle's class are off on a school trip to the funfair. But when they arrive, there are some very strange characters hanging around. Could they have anything to do with the spate of robberies that have been happening around town? Lee, Billy and Bella decide to do some investigation and get to the bottom of the mystery.